EZRA DAWN

The Keeper's Lost Love
Ezra Dawn

Cover art created by JeB Designs
jebdesigns@outlook.com

TABLE OF

CHARACTER NAME
Pronunciation

Ferris VanAllen (Fair-ris, Van-Allen)

Laken Key (Lay-ken, Key)

FOREIGN

Sydämeni – Finnish for my heart

Rakkaani - Finnish for my love

Mini Author's Note: Valtameri is a completely fictional location in Finland named after the Finnish word for ocean.

ABOUT THE

(The Keeper's Lost Love is a short story with the instalove of fated mates. It is a complete standalone.)

Ferris VanAllen has been the lighthouse keeper on the coast of the Valtameri peninsula in Finland for fifteen years having taken over from his ailing grandfather. Vacationing on Valtameri in the summer was always one of Ferris' favorite things growing up. At least, until the summer he turned seventeen and the boy he'd been in love with suddenly disappeared, never to be seen or heard from again.

Laken Key is a narwhal shifter who lived on Valtameri with his blessing. As a teenager, he'd been in love with the human boy who lived by the lighthouse. They were inseparable and he'd hoped they were fated mates but wouldn't know for sure until his eighteenth birthday. Only Laken never got the chance to find out. Captured by other humans while shifted and swimming of the coast, Laken was taken away.

Now, twenty years later, the boy Ferris once knew has become a man and he's coming home. Laken fears what he'll find when he returns but he decides to face it head on. Ferris has spent years wondering what happened to Laken and why he disappeared. Can Laken undo the heartbreak Ferris has felt over the last twenty years or will he be too late to stop Ferris from giving his heart to someone else?

(**Warning:** Contains graphic sexual content and explicit language. Not recommended for those under the age of 18.)

PROLOGUE

Twenty Years Ago...

Meet me at our spot

7 PM Tonight

Xoxo

Laken

Reading over the note Laken left under a rock on my windowsill, I smile and head for the shower across the hall from my bedroom. I've been helping my grandfather do regular maintenance on the lighthouse today and I stink. I don't know what Laken has planned for our date tonight, but I'd rather not show up smelling like sweat and grease. I originally wanted to plan our date since it's Laken's birthday today and I wanted to do something special for him, but Laken refused, stating he already had a plan in mind. So, I let it go instead of fighting him on it.

Laken and I have been friends since we were ten and I started spending summers here on Valtameri with my grandfather while my parents jettisoned around the world. It was only in the last two years that our friendship turned to more and I couldn't be happier. Sure, the long-distance part has been frustrating, but it all fades away when summer rolls around. I'll be eighteen soon and when that happens, I can finally move here permanently and be with Laken all the time. *I can't wait.* My parents want me to go to college and get a business degree so I can take over my dad's company but it's not what I want. They'll probably cut me off, but I don't care. I'll gladly get a job if it means I can stay here and be happy.

After my shower, I dress in a short sleeve button down shirt and my nicest pair of cargo shorts. Slipping my feet into a pair of sandals, I call out, "Grandpa, I'm going to meet Laken," and head for the front door. It's poker night, so I know grandpa won't be too lonely without me here to keep him company.

Grandpa shouts, "Have fun and don't stay out too late."

"I won't!"

Leaving the house, I make my way down the path to the beach. There's a small private inlet with a cave that Laken and I discovered when we were younger. It's become our spot and where we spend most of our time when we want to be alone together. I enjoy listening to the ocean waves breaking on the shore and the smell of salt in the air. This place calls to me and I hate going back to the city at the end of summer.

When I reach the cave, I'm surprised to see Laken isn't here. I check my watch. It's already seven. I'd expected a romantic scene, like a picnic complete with candles but there's nothing. Thinking he got held up doing something for his family, I decide to wait. One hour, turns to two and then three before I finally admit to myself that he isn't coming. Disappointment shrouds me as I make my way back home, but it turns to heartbreak the next day when I learn Laken has disappeared, and no one knows where he's gone.

Was this your plan, Laken?

CHAPTER ONE

Walking into my grandfather's room, I say, "Good morning, Grandpa, I brought you breakfast," then put his breakfast tray on the rolling table by his bed. Pressing the button on the side of his bed, I raise the top of the bed so he's sitting up then tuck some pillows behind his back to make him comfortable. Rolling the table into place in front of him, I remove the lid covering the plate with a flourish and in a fake French accent tell him, "Today we have for you a croque monsieur, scrambled eggs, and a café au lait with a side of fresh strawberries drizzled in dark chocolate. Enjoy, monsieur."

My antics get a chuckle from him, and I smile. Grandpa had a stroke recently and is completely paralyzed on his left side. Speaking isn't easy for him anymore either. It takes him a bit longer to put his thoughts into words and sometimes he isn't able to understand what I'm saying to him. I refused to let my parents put him in a home like they wanted when it happened so, when I'm not taking care of the lighthouse, I'm caring for grandpa with the help of the nurse I hired. Leaving him to enjoy his breakfast, I head downstairs. Michelle, the nurse is just pulling in the driveway, so I step out onto the porch and wave at her.

She exits her car and I try not to laugh at her poop emoji scrubs. She's always wearing scrubs with crazy designs, and they never fail to make me want to laugh. Michelle is a tiny sprite of a woman with the strength of a man. The first time I saw her pick up my grandfather and put him in his wheelchair like he weighed nothing my jaw hit the floor. "Good morning Michelle. Grandpa is having breakfast. I'll be doing some repairs on the light in the lighthouse if you need me for anything."

Michelle grins at me and says teasingly, "I never do. I'll call you when it's time for lunch so you can eat with him."

Nodding, I hug her and walk away from the house climbing the stone steps to the lighthouse up on the cliffside. Valtameri is a peninsula attached to Finland. It's small and home to roughly one thousand people. There are tons of rocks along and off the shoreline where the lighthouse stands. The lighthouse was built in 1783 and fully automated in

1998. It's a tall solid white brick structure with a lantern room made from glass and black steel. Inside the lighthouse, pictures, and news articles line the walls as you ascend to the lantern room depicting the history of the lighthouse and its caretakers. There's artwork too, from multiple artists spanning generations who used the lighthouse as their muse. This place is a piece of history and I love everything about it.

The caretaker's house isn't as old as the lighthouse is because it's been torn down and rebuilt multiple times over the years. Sometimes it was due to a major storm damaging the building's integrity and other times it was due to the size of the caretaker's family. The house started as a simple one-bedroom shack and is now a large cape style house with five bedrooms and four and a half bathrooms. It's the perfect size for a family and has always been my dream house. Growing up and spending my summers here I knew this was where I'd live for the rest of my life once I found someone to settle down with. I thought I'd found that someone twenty years ago, but I was wrong.

After Laken disappeared, I avoided Valtameri for a while. I went to college and got the degree my parents wanted me to get. My dad wanted me to start in his company and work my way up from the bottom, so I'd learn everything about the business, and I agreed, even though working there is the last thing I ever wanted to do. I'd been working as an intern for a year when grandpa had a bad fall off a ladder and broke his leg in three places. He'd been trying to repair some damage to the roof of the house after a storm hit. When I got the news that he'd been hurt, I dropped everything and rushed to Valtameri to help him.

Spending time on Valtameri brought back a lot of memories and reminded me of how much I loved the place. So, even when grandpa was feeling better and back to his old self, I didn't leave. Instead, I quit my job, packed up all my things, and moved here permanently where I took over Grandpa's duties so he could retire. Which he did, for the most part. Before the stroke, I'd still catch him trying to do things around the property. I felt like a parent catching their child reaching into the cookie jar before dinner every time. My parents are still pissed at me for my decision and completely cut me off. Thankfully, when I quit, I'd already gained access to my trust fund so, even though being the lighthouse caretaker doesn't pay much, I'm able to pay for grandpa's care.

Members of our family have been caretakers of the lighthouse for generations. We own the land and the lighthouse but because it's a necessary fixture that protects the ships coming into port, the government pays us to keep it operational. Had I not fallen in love with the lighthouse, and Valtameri like I did, the legacy would've ended with my grandfather. I don't like thinking of him dying, but I know it'll happen sooner or later. I'm hoping for later. Grandpa is eighty-five and I want another ten or twenty years with him still around. I'd like for him to be there when I get married and start a family. Though I'd have to date someone long enough for any of that to happen. I've gone on plenty of dates, but nothing ever comes from them. Deep down, I know nothing ever will because even after twenty years, I'm still hung up on Laken.

My friends try setting me up all the time. They tell me I need to move on. That Laken likely died swimming in the ocean that day, and I need to accept it. No one as close to his family as he was, willingly disappears and goes years without contacting them at some point. In my head, I know they're right but, in my heart, I feel like he's out there somewhere. Alive. Maybe it's stupid, but I can't shake the feeling. Like somehow my soul knows it's true.

I know, it's not good for me to pine after someone who's long gone if I want to have the future I've dreamed of, with a partner and kids. But I can't help it. Laken was the love of my life, and no one can ever compare. Believe me, I've tried seeing other people. It's inevitable that I make the comparison and they never measure up. Sometimes, I wonder if I'm sabotaging relationships on purpose because I'm afraid of having my heart broken again. Then I wonder if I built up everything I felt with Laken in my head to the point where no one compares because they're competing with a fantasy.

Maybe it's because I never got real closure, or maybe it's because I never stopped loving Laken. Whatever the reason, I can't let go and move on no matter how hard I've tried. I should probably come to terms with the fact I'll never have someone to share my life with unless Laken magically comes back from the dead and if I want kids, I'll have to pay a surrogate myself and do it on my own. Sighing, I shake off those melancholy thoughts and head inside the lighthouse. I grab my tool bag and the box containing the part I need from the storage closet at the base of the stairs then make my way up to the lantern room.

The automatic lamp changer is on the fritz and the replacement finally arrived last night. I was out on a date with Stanley, so I didn't get the chance to install it. I can't have the light on while I work on the mechanism that automatically changes the bulbs when one burns out. Stanley is one of the many men my friends have set me up with. He's a nice guy and I like talking to him which is why I haven't ended things with him even though I should. We've been going out on dates once a week for the past two months and haven't gone further than kissing. Stanley has been hinting at me spending the night with him, but I haven't agreed. There's no spark between us and if I'm honest with myself, I feel nothing for him beyond friendship. It would be cruel to continue to lead him on when I know in my heart this won't be going anywhere.

As if my thoughts summoned him, my phone starts ringing in my pocket. Shifting the box and tool bag to one side, I grab my phone. Stanley's name flashes across the screen and I answer it.

"Hello?"

"Hey gorgeous, I was wondering if you'd like to come over for dinner tonight at my place? I'm making seafood lasagna."

Damn...that's my favorite but I can't say yes just to eat the food.

"I don't think that's a good idea."

"Why not? You've had dinner here before. Though I'll admit, this time I'm hoping you'll stay over instead of leaving after a movie."

Sighing, I say, "Stanley, you're a great guy and a good friend but I don't see us being more than that. I thought if I gave it more time, my feelings would change but I was wrong, and I can't continue to lead you on. I'm sorry. The truth is I lost my heart to someone a long time ago and I never got it back."

Stanley sighs and tells me, "I can't say I'm not disappointed. I really do like you, and I was hoping we could be more. You've been putting distance between us since I first asked you to spend the night. It was an obvious sign that you weren't on the same page as me. So, in a way, I knew this was coming."

"I'm sorry."

"Don't be, I get it. You can't build a relationship on something that isn't there. My invitation for dinner still stands if you want to join me as a friend and not a boyfriend. In fact, I'll invite the guys and we'll make it a group thing."

His words bring a smile to my face, and it's a relief knowing he's going to be okay. I don't like hurting people so, I'm glad we're able to continue as friends. "Sounds like a plan, I'll be there."

"See you at seven then."

Ending the call, I put the phone back in my pocket then continue up the stairs to the lantern room. *Time to work.*

CHAPTER TWO

"Laken come on! The water's great."

Barking out a laugh, I shout, "Says the guy who screamed like a girl about how cold it is when he got in!"

Ferris grins at me and says, "It's better now that I'm used to it. Have I ever steered you wrong?"

Tapping my chin with a finger, I tell him, "Well there was that one time..."

Ferris laughs, "Shut up and get in here. I promise it's not that bad!"

Grinning, I whip off my shirt and kick off my sandals then head for the water. When my toes hit the frigid surf, I gasp and shout, "You little liar! It's fucking cold!"

I'm pulled from the memory by the sound of shouting. The words get lost in the storm that's been raging all day long. Outside my tank the curiosity show employees are racing around trying to take things down and load up as quickly as possible. I've been stuck in this tank in my narwhal form for twenty years. I'm able to keep track of time passing thanks to the giant sign banners advertising the show that are within viewing distance of the tank I'm being kept in.

They captured me when I was swimming off the coast of Valtameri. I'd gone to calm my nerves about the date I had planned that night. It was my eighteenth birthday which meant I could finally confirm the suspicions I had about Ferris being my fated mate. Shifters might gain their animal forms at puberty but we're unable to recognize mates by scent until we've reached adulthood. Fear that I was wrong about him being my mate comingled with the fear of how he'd react to the news that I wasn't human had me frazzled and on edge.

It's why I never saw them coming. One minute I was swimming along minding my own business and the next I was caught in a net, hauled onto a boat, and injected with something that knocked me out. I came to in a tank on the boat with no means of escape because the tank was chained down and only had a small sliding window cut into the top where my food was dropped through. I was smuggled here, wherever *here* is, and I've been part of this curiosity show ever since. When I first ended up here, I tried to escape but it didn't work. I don't know where they got it or how they knew about me being a shifter, but they put something in my tank water that trapped me in this form. It's been so long since I was able to shift, I sometimes worry my human side will disappear completely and leave only the animal behind.

After that failure of a first escape attempt, I haven't tried again. With the drugs and the way my tank is built, escape is impossible. My tank is an oval racetrack type that's as wide as the length of my body and only a few feet longer than I am. It restricts my movements so I'm only able to swim the racetrack shape. There's air holes cut into the lid, but it stays padlocked shut. The only time it's opened is when I'm being fed or dosed with the drug. They know I won't try anything because as a narwhal, even if I did make it out of the tank, I wouldn't be able to go anywhere until the drug wore off. By the time it did, someone would've noticed I was out, and I'd be right back in the tank where I started.

The tank is glass and I'm sure I could break it with my horn if I could build enough speed and hit it. Sadly, the people running this show must've taken all possible avenues of escape into consideration because this tank isn't anywhere near the size I would need in order to build enough speed to break the glass. At this point, I've resigned myself to my fate. I'll spend the rest of my life in a tank being gawked at by curious humans. Sometimes I wish I could die so I'd be free of this place and can wait for Ferris to join me in the afterlife.

With Ferris being human, I wouldn't have to wait long. *Gods, I miss him.* Memories of the summers we spent together and the love we had for each other are the only things keeping me from losing myself completely. I long to be able to reunite with him but it's a pipe dream. A fantasy. It's been so long, I'm sure he's moved on and forgotten all about me. Maybe he's married with a couple kids and living in the caretaker's house, taking care of the lighthouse like he always planned. Or maybe, my disappearance destroyed the love he had for Valtameri and he's working some corporate job in a big city for the family company like his dad wanted. I can torture myself with what-ifs, but I'll never know the answer to the questions.

The lid to my tank opens and I raise my head above the water so I can get my meal. Only, it doesn't come. Instead, I hear one of the other show employees shouting, "There's a flash flood warning for this area, we've got to go, now!"

The employee holding my tank lid open shouts, "What about the animals?"

"We've loaded all the ones we can. The big tanks are going to take too much time. Drop some food in them, seal the tanks and let's go. We'll come back for the remaining animals after the storm passes."

The guy holding my tank lid up shrugs and says, "Okay," then dumps a bucket of squid and shrimp into the tank with me.

The lid falls shut, and I focus on filling my belly. It's fucking humiliating being reduced to relying on someone else to feed me, but I've gotten used to it. By the time I've finished my meal, the fairgrounds where the curiosity show set up are deserted. Left behind are some banners, some trash, and a few other tanks. One houses a giant saltwater croc, one has a vaquita, and the final tank holds a pair of pink river dolphins. All of us are shifters. I know because I've seen the employees dump the same powder, they put in my tank in theirs. Shifters or not, some of our animal halves are rare. You'd think a curiosity show with a number of captive endangered species would be shut down by some marine wildlife conservation place but somehow the show owners have managed to get away with it.

As I'm scarfing down the last bit of squid, I hear a roaring sound seconds before a massive five-foot wall of muddy water slams into my tank, washing it away. I spot the other tanks floating along with the water that is pushing us toward a group of trees. As the trees get closer, I close my eyes and wait for the impact. Minutes later, the tank slams into a large tree and shatters. Glass shards embed in my skin, but I can't find it in myself to care because I'm free. The shattering of more glass tells me the other tanks have broken too. Letting the current created by the floodwaters carry me away, I pray it'll take me out to sea so I can find my way home again. Or, at the very least, go far enough that the drugs will wear off so I can shift and find someone to help me get home.

The latter would be better since the motion of swimming will keep the wounds from healing around the glass shards and I have no desire to tempt any sharks with my blood. Hearing a splash to my left, I look over and see the river dolphins keeping pace at my side with the saltwater croc drifting along on their left. I don't see the vaquita and I'm worried they didn't make it through the tank breaking. *Such a fucking shame.* The four of us sticking together until we can shift is a good idea. There's strength in numbers and we're all vulnerable right now. Once we're able to shift we can find someplace to hide and figure out what our next move will be.

Hours later, I feel my human half stirring in the back of my mind and it's a huge relief to know I haven't lost that side of myself completely. Knowing I should be able to shift now, I swim for higher ground with the others following right behind me. The croc passes me reaching land first and shifts. He's a tall brickhouse of a man with long blond hair and bears a striking resemblance to an armored blond man with a hammer I saw on a human's t-shirt once. The river dolphins shift into short rail thin identical twins with light pink hair that's an odd contrast to their darkly tanned skin. The larger man helps them ashore then turns his attention to me after saying something to the twins I don't catch. Before I can shift, all three of them grab hold of me and lift me out of the water.

The large man says in an Australian accent, "Don't shift yet, mate. We're going to pull this glass out first. Some of these shards are large and you don't want them travelling when you shift and injure something vital."

Nodding my understanding, I force myself to remain still so they can work. The agony of the shards being removed makes me want to throw up and pass out at the same time. When the last shard is gone, I immediately shift knowing it'll speed up the healing of the wounds, so I won't continue to bleed like a stuck pig. Breathing heavily, I look up at the three men and say, "Thank you."

"You're welcome."

Looking at the water as it rushes past, I ask, "Did anyone see where the vaquita went?"

The twins both flinch and my heart sinks. In a broken whisper, one of the twins says, "Their tank was in between ours and the tree we collided with. They didn't stand a chance."

Unable to resist the urge to comfort them, I give them a hug, deliberately ignoring the fact that we're all naked. "Fuck, I'm so sorry. That must've been terrible to witness."

They nod, and step back. "Are either of you hurt?"

The twins shake their heads. "No. We made it through fine."

I raise an eyebrow at the large man, and he says, "I'm unharmed as well. Your tank was a lot smaller than either of ours."

I know he's right. Their tanks were a lot bigger than mine. The size difference is likely the reason I got hit with glass shards and they didn't. I hate that the vaquita didn't make it. Now their family will never know what happened to them. It's awful and it pisses me off. I swear, as soon as the opportunity arises, I'll get someone to see to the shutdown and arrest of the curiosity show owners. We're not the only paranormals they had and someone has to rescue them. I'd also like to know how they found out about our world and where they got the drug that kept us from shifting. *Answers I'll be sure to get another day.*

The large man looks around and says, "Come on, let's find some place to get clothes. We can't be going around naked."

One of the twins points and says, "There's some houses over there. I'm sure we can find one where the owners aren't home."

The large man—I really need to get his name—nods and starts walking toward the neighborhood. We stick to the woods, so we aren't spotted by any neighbors. The gods must be smiling on us because the first house we come to is empty and the backdoor is unlocked. The house belongs to a large family judging by the pictures lining the walls and the wide range of toys scattered across the living room. It takes us fifteen minutes to find clothes that somewhat fit, including shoes and another five for the twins to find a bag and toss some food into it to take with us. There isn't any way to know how long it'll take for the water to recede. We might be on our own for a while before we find someone to help us.

While the twins are busy and the large man keeps watch for the family returning, I search for something we can use to figure out where we are. We don't want to linger too long and end up getting spotted and reported to the authorities, so I have to find something quickly. Spotting a stack of mail on a table, I rush over and pick up the first envelope I come to. *Holy shit...we're in Texas.* The twins say,

"Hey horned fish guy, we've got the food packed so let's get out of here."

The way they said that in unison is a tad bit creepy, but the horned fish guy comment has me fighting back a laugh. I return the envelope to the table and follow them to the back door. The Australian—because that's a bit better than calling him large man—hands out a couple umbrellas he must've found while keeping watch for the family returning. Now, we don't have to worry about getting our dry clothes wet with the rain still coming down in a torrent. Umbrellas in hand, we step out onto the back patio and raise them then head for the woods at a hurried pace since the umbrellas are like a beacon that'll get us spotted if we aren't careful.

When we're safely ensconced in the trees, the twins ask, "So, what now?"

The Australian says, "Now, we go looking for some help. I think if we follow the water or the unflooded roads, we'll find a town. Hopefully, we'll run into someone like us who can help. If not, we might have to steal a map and see if we can figure out how to get back to our homes from here."

Looking at the three of them, I say, "The second option might be difficult. At least for me. We're in Texas. Midland to be specific. We'd have to find our way to the coast and trust that our animal halves knew how to get us back home. That's if we could handle swimming thousands of miles in one shot. I don't know about the three of you, but I don't think my animal half would do well in the warmer ocean water of the gulf."

The twins nod in agreement. "He has a point. We wouldn't be able to swim in the ocean. Our animal halves can only survive in freshwater."

The Australian scrubs a hand over his face and sighs. "Okay, that nixes that plan for anyone but me. We'll focus on finding a town and someone like us to help. They'll be able to contact this continent's council for us."

One of the twins says, "Well if we're going to be traveling together, I think we should at least know each other's names. I'm Jaco and this is my brother Jordao."

Raising my hand, I tell them, "I'm Laken."

The Australian says, "Oscar."

Jaco smiles. "It's nice to meet all of you."

"You too."

Jordao asks, "Alright, which way are we heading?"

Oscar points in the direction the water is flowing and says, "Let's head that way until we find a road that isn't under water we can follow to a town."

Jaco salutes him. "Lead on captain."

Laughing, I shake my head and follow the three of them. After an hour of walking, we come to a town. There doesn't seem to be many people out and about because of the rain and flooding so we head into the closest store. It's a little quick mart attached to a gas station. There're only a few people inside. Two customers and the cashier. Oscar heads right for the tall man in the candy aisle who reminds me of Lurch from *The Addams Family*, if Lurch was a dark haired adonis dressed in biker leather.

The vest he's wearing has a wicked looking patch on the back. It's a skull wearing a knight's helmet in front of crossed halberds and a shield. Another patch above it says Grim Knights and another one below it says Texas. I can't scent him from here because even heightened my sense of smell isn't that good, but I'm certain the man in leather is a paranormal. Oscar wouldn't have approached him if he wasn't. *Unless he was Oscar's mate.*

After a brief conversation, Oscar drags the man over to us and says, "Guys, this is Widow, he's going to help us."

CHAPTER THREE

With a twelve pack of beer and a bottle of wine in hand, I ring Stanley's doorbell. The Volvo my friends usually drive is parked behind Stanley's Volkswagen. Stanley lives in a two-bedroom cottage in a suburban neighborhood twenty minutes from the lighthouse. Of course, I'm the last one to arrive. My friends are used to me being habitually late by now. I tend to lose track of time when I'm in my shop. The lighthouse doesn't need a ton of work daily since I stay on top of things so when I finish my task list there, I'm usually in my shop blowing glass.

After quitting my corporate job and hiring Michelle to help with grandpa, I needed something to fill the hours when I found myself with nothing to do. I saw an advertisement for a free introductory glass blowing class being held by the art institute and decided it wouldn't hurt to check it out. It was the best decision I ever made. The class sparked a passion in me, and I signed up for more classes. Three years later, I graduated with a master's degree in fine arts and had my own workshop built on the property.

My friend Michael is a graphic designer. His focus is usually book covers but he helped me get a website and online store set up to sell my pieces. Michael's husband James is a marketing genius and took care of advertising for me. I've got plenty of orders rolling in that'll keep me occupied. I was working on a commissioned dolphin sculpture. It's a large piece and getting the waves just right is the reason I'm late.

Michael opens the door and I step inside. The smell of seafood lasagna immediately hits me in the face and my mouth waters. Michael slaps me on the back and says with a boisterous laugh, "Someone's late to the party. But I see you brought booze, so you're forgiven," then he swipes the bottle of wine from me and heads into Stanley's kitchen. Stanley is at counter putting together a salad while a timer with five minutes remaining ticks down on the oven. James is seated at the island with a glass of something pink that is so bright it's practically glowing. The color matches the skintight silk t-shirt and glittery sneakers he's wearing. Eyeing the glass warily, I ask, "What kind of drink is that?"

James turns to me, and his equally pink lips tilt up in a grin. "It's called a pink poodle. It's good you should try it."

Chuckling, I shake my head. "No thanks. I'll pass. You know how I get with cocktails that taste good. Especially, if I can't taste the alcohol in them. Last time I drank one of your cocktails it was Halloween and let's just say it didn't end well."

James' green eyes light up with curiosity and I know I won't get out of telling him the whole story. I'm in for some serious ribbing. Setting the beer on the counter, I pull one from the box, open it and take a sip. Parking my ass on one of the barstools, I turn to James and continue the story. "You were on that business trip and Michael made those green cocktails from the recipe you suggested. I don't recall how many I had but I woke up underneath your coffee table in nothing but a tutu and tights, clinging to a bowl of candy like it held the secrets of the universe and Michael's feet were in my face."

Laughing at the memory, I go on, "He'd passed out while sitting on the couch still wearing his nutcracker costume. There was a lollipop stick stuck to his chin, melted chocolate in his hair and a half-eaten candy bar enclosed in the fist resting on his chest like he'd been in the middle of eating it when he passed out."

James throws his head back and laughs. "I wish I'd been there to see that."

Stanley's shoulders are shaking as he slices a cucumber and I know he's stifling his laughter. Michael grumbling as he searches Stanley's drawers for a corkscrew only makes me laugh harder. Stanley finishes the salad and turns, leaning back against the counter. His eyes dance with mirth when he asks, "So, whose idea was it to dress up as characters from The Nutcracker?"

Michael and I both point to James and he laughs. James sips his pink poodle and says, "I was given tickets to the ballet as a thank you from a client. The day after seeing it, we started the discussion of coordinating costumes, and it was the first thing that came to mind."

The oven timer beeps, and Stanley pulls the lasagna from the oven. Michael helps him plate the food and we move to the dining table to eat. The food is delicious, and the conversation revolves around work and funny stories. I switch to drinking water halfway through the meal since I'm going to drive home. Hours later, after helping Stanley clean up, I walk out of the house with Michael. James is already passed out in the passenger seat of their car having had one too many pink poodles. Michael came back in to get the to-go bag of leftovers.

As we're walking toward the cars, Michael asks, "So, how are things going with you and Stanley? You guys have been dating a couple months now, right? Why not spend the night?"

I've managed to avoid this topic all night, but it seems Michael isn't going to let me avoid it any longer. If James weren't passed out in the car, he'd be right here with Michael asking the same probing questions. Running my fingers through my hair, I tell him, "Stanley and I have decided we're better friends than lovers. Stanley took it surprisingly well when I told him I didn't have romantic feelings for him."

Michael sighs in frustration. "This again? Come on, Ferris. You can't still be hung up on Laken. I know James and I never met him, so we have no way to know if what you guys had was as real as you're convinced it was, but it's been twenty years. You can't continue to live your life pining over a man who is either dead or off living his best life somewhere else likely with someone else because he was too much of a coward to end things with you to your face."

His words send a shaft of pain through me. It's not a new argument but it still hurts. In my heart, I know *I know* Laken never would've left without saying goodbye like that unless something bad happened to him. But we were so close, so in love, I'd know if he were dead. I'd feel it. He's out there somewhere. But I can't let myself think of where he might be and what he's doing because there's the slim chance that Michael is right. It would kill me to find out Laken's been living it up somewhere while I've been stuck here, pining over him.

Michael squeezes my shoulder and says, "I'm sorry, I've upset you, but you can't keep going on like this. James and I want to see you happy and settled. You shouldn't have to live your life alone because you're hanging on to a ghost. Just think about it. I love you man."

Hugging him, I say, "I love you too. Get your lush of a husband home before those pink poodles make a reappearance."

Michael laughs and heads for his Volvo. I wave at him as he drives past me then cross to where I parked my own vehicle. Climbing in, I rest my head against the seat and close my eyes for a minute as the weight of Michael's words push down on me. I love him and James but neither of them understand. Laken was my everything and I can't just let him go. I've tried. It never works.

Breathing out, I put the keys in the ignition and start the engine. Pulling a U-Turn, I make my way home. When I get there, I immediately head to grandpa's room to check on him. Michelle is gone for the night and grandpa is sound asleep. He has a routine so he's usually out for the night by nine so it's safe for Michelle to leave even if I'm not here. Seeing that he's fine, I walk to my own room. Flipping on the light, I walk over to the window and raise it. I like sleeping with it open so I can hear the waves crash against the shore and smell the salt in the air.

I close it before I leave for the day. Valtameri's crime rate is virtually nonexistent but I'm not going to take any chances on leaving it open, not when my grandpa can't defend himself from an intruder. With the window raised, I run my fingers over the rock that's been there since the last time Laken left me a note. Whispering, "I miss you," like I always do every night before bed, I back away from the window. Stripping out of my clothes, I turn out the light and crawl into bed. Closing my eyes, I let sleep take me so I can see Laken in my dreams.

CHAPTER FOUR

Breathing in deep as I step outside the airport, I smile happily. Pulling out my new cell phone, I open the group chat I have with Oscar, Jaco, Jordao and Widow. Typing out a text, I hit send.

Me: Landed.

Oscar, Jaco, and Jordao are likely still in the air, but Widow will get the message. When he said he'd help us, he wasn't kidding. Widow is a member of a motorcycle club made up almost entirely of gay paranormals. Widow found a rental place and secured a vehicle for us with a trailer to tow his bike and we made our way to San Antonio where his club's based, avoiding flooded areas along the way. The club reported our situation to the council and filmed our statements of what happened to us so we could get back home as soon as possible without having to wait until the council could send a representative to conduct interviews.

A member of Widow's club named Classified created identity papers for each of us, including fake passports to allow us passage out of the country and a guy named Tinker gave us cell phones he'd made himself that pull service from satellites and are completely untraceable. After a lesson in how to use them, Widow then took us shopping for some clothes and luggage bags to carry them in. Once we had everything we needed, Widow bought our plane tickets and saw us off at the airport. All in all, we only spent about eight hours with the club, but it was long enough to consider them lifelong friends. I know if I ever need help, I can call on them. I've got the name and number of every Grim Knights member across all charters stored in my phone thanks to Widow.

Shifting my bag higher on my shoulder, I hail a cab to take me to Valtameri. The fare is going to be outrageous because the nearest airport to Valtameri is Helsinki-Malmi, a full seventy-five miles away. Thankfully, Widow gave me some cash to use. I had it turned into Euro at the little exchange machine as soon as I disembarked from the plane. So, I've got enough to cover the fare. I've been in the air for thirteen hours and dawn is just breaking. The first person I want to see is Ferris but I'm terrified. I was so worried about what I'd find here that I hardly slept on the plane. I have to know even if I'm scared of it. So, my plan is to leave Ferris a note like I've always done and wait for him to join me at our spot. I don't want to knock on the door in case he has a family.

Inside the cab, I give the driver the address of the local market on Valtameri Ferris and I would go to for a bag full of candies as kids. After an hour of driving, I pay the cabbie and wait for him to turn around before I start walking to the lighthouse. Even in the early morning hours, the beacon still shines. The sun is halfway risen when I arrive at my destination. The trellis I always climbed to reach Ferris' window is still intact. Leaving my bag on the ground, I climb up it to the open window. Slipping the note I wrote on a napkin during the flight from my pocket, I leave it under the rock.

I'll be waiting at our spot

Come find me

Laken

It's doesn't even come close to all the things I want to say to him. But, I felt explanations would be better in person so, I kept it simple. A faint snore draws my attention to the bed. A shock of brown hair sticks out from a cocoon of blankets. I'm tempted to climb through the window and get a closer look at the person sleeping in the bed, *is it Ferris, or someone else* but I force myself to climb back down the trellis instead. Picking up my bag, I walk down the path to our spot.

Using the flashlight on my phone to light the way, I enter the cave. It's just like I remember it only there're a few new additions. Toward the back of the cave where the tides don't reach is a stone firepit next to a comfortable looking chair. The cave is at an incline on higher ground, so when it's high tide, the water goes midway into the cave. Making my way to the chair, I drop my bag in the sand and use the supplies by the pit to start a fire. When I've got it going, I sit down in the chair and wait for Ferris.

On the flight here, I went over multiple scenarios of what would happen when I met up with Ferris again. Out of all of them, only one was in my favor. In the first, he was so angry about the way I'd disappeared and left him behind he wouldn't give me the time of day and feels I should've stayed away. In the second, he was married with kids and while he appreciated the gesture of giving him closure, he'd rather we be friends. The third is how I'm hoping things will go. With Ferris listening to my explanation and having enough love for me still in his heart, we can pick up where we left off. Though this option is contingent on us being mates. If he isn't meant to be mine, I don't know what I'll do.

My phone dings multiple times and I look at the screen.

Widow: Glad you arrived safely.

Jaco & Jordao: Just landed too.

Oscar: I'm stuck in Miami. Bird strike fucked up one of the engines, so the plane was forced to make an emergency landing. The next flight out to Australia isn't until mid-day tomorrow so I'll be spending the rest of the night here.

Widow *replying to Oscar*: I know a guy with a private jet. He's a pilot and part of the Tallahassee charter if you don't want to wait for another flight. Name's Maverick. You'll find his number in your phone.

Oscar *replying to Widow*: Calling him now, thanks.

Jaco: *pouty face emoji* I want to ride on a private jet.

Jordao: Samesies.

Chuckling, I shake my head and type out a reply.

> **Me**: Have fun on your flight, Oscar. I hear private planes are fancy.

"Laken?"

The deep voice, full of emotion coming from in front of me has me jerking my head up. Ferris is standing there, in nothing but a pair of pajama pants and two different shoes like he hurried from the house as soon as he got my note. He's not the lanky boy I remember. Ferris has grown into a man, stacked with muscle and covered in ink. His face is a bit more rugged, with light brown stubble and a pillow mark on his cheek. The eyes and that messy brown hair are the same. Those eyes are wet with unshed tears and he's shaking.

Rising from the chair, I hold out my arms and say, "Hello *sydämeni*." The term of endearment rolls off my tongue with ease and as soon as it leaves my lips, Ferris launches himself at me. He hugs me so tight, it's difficult to breathe but I'm not about to say anything. Having him in my arms again is a dream come true and I don't want it to end anytime soon. Burying my face into his neck, I inhale his scent of sea salt, pine, and something uniquely him and nearly moan out loud. *I was right...he is mine. Thank the gods.*

Ferris' shoulders shake under my hands and a wet spot is forming on my t-shirt where he's buried his face into my shoulder. Rubbing his back, I comfort him silently, giving him all the time he needs to get himself back together. When he finally steps back, eyes red from crying, he says, "I can't believe it's you. That you're really here. When I saw that note I thought it was one of my friends playing a cruel joke on me. I came here thinking I'd find an empty cave. Like before."

The raw pain in his eyes cuts me to the core. Taking his face between my hands, I tell him, "I'm sorry I wasn't here, *sydämeni*. That my absence caused you pain."

Ferris grips my wrists and rubs circles with his thumbs. "Why weren't you here? Where have you been for the past twenty years?"

"In order for you to understand the answers to those questions, I'll have to show you something first."

"Anything. Show me."

Stepping away from him, I say, "Come with me," and walk toward the mouth of the cave. Once outside, I stop at the edge of the beach and turn to face Ferris.

"Before I show you, I want you to know that I'd never hurt you, that I'm still me and I recognize you."

Ferris says, "Okay," sounding a little skeptical. Knowing I need to get this over with, I start stripping.

Ferris' eyes widen and heat, "Why are you getting naked?"

Winking at him, I say, "You'll see," and finish undressing. Once I'm naked, I remind him, "Remember, I'm still me," and initiate my shift. I'm hoping the fact he loved reading paranormal romances as a teenager will make this easier to accept.

When my transformation is complete, Ferris' eyes are wide with shock and his pupils are huge. "Holy shit. You're a shifter! Shifters are real. Does that mean everything else I've read about is real too?" Ferris' breath starts coming faster and he fans himself with his hand. I can sense his rising panic and if he doesn't calm down, he's going to pass out. I've overwhelmed him with everything, and I can't help but think I should've eased him into this a bit more instead of springing it on him all at once. Me reappearing after twenty years and shaking up his world with my return was a shock in itself. Add in the news paranormals are real and I'm kind of surprised he's still standing here right now and hasn't taken off running for the hills.

Shifting back, I nod and say, "It's all real, *sydämeni*. Though there are some things in the stories that aren't true."

I don't know how it's possible for his eyes to widen even more with his shock, but they do. "Are fated mates one of those untrue things?" There's something hesitant in his eyes when he asks, as if he's afraid of the answer. His voice has gone high-pitched and squeaky. I think it's adorable, but his face turns red with embarrassment.

Pulling on my clothes, I shake my head. "No. Fated mates are a very real thing. And you, are mine." *And there he goes...*Ferris' eyes roll back into his head, and he falls backward onto the sand. *I probably should've kept my mouth shut on that one.* Sitting next to his prone form, I wait for him to wake up.

When Ferris comes to a couple minutes later, he rubs his hands over his face, and turns to me looking like he's about to cry again. "I think now's a good time for that explanation. If we're mates, I've got to know why you'd abandon me for twenty years."

Pacing back and forth I explain, "I didn't know for sure we were mates back then though I did suspect it. For shifters, we don't gain the ability to scent our mates until we're adults. Which is usually around the age of eighteen. I didn't leave on purpose.

I'd planned to bring you here and show you my animal form after we'd had a picnic dinner."

"So, what happened? Why weren't you there?"

Turning to face him, I give him a sad smile and tell him, "I was nervous about how the night would go so I decided to go for a swim in my narwhal form to clear my head. One minute, I was swimming along and the next, I was caught in a net and hauled onto a boat. They hit me with a sedative and when I came to, I was in a tank that was chained shut aboard the boat."

Ferris covers his mouth with his hand, his expression horrified. Needing to get all of this out, I continue, "I was sold to a curiosity show and I wasn't the only one. Somehow, they knew what we were. We were drugged so we couldn't shift back to our human forms and were given no means of escape. If a flash flood warning hadn't made them leave all their aquatic shifters behind only for us to be washed away in it and if we hadn't met Widow, we'd all still be there."

Ferris pulls me into a hug and says, "I'm so sorry that happened to you but I'm glad you got away. In my heart, I always knew you wouldn't leave me like that, and I knew you couldn't be dead because I would've felt it. My friends have been telling me for years I needed to move on and let go of you, but I couldn't. Now I know why that is and why no one else ever compared to you. We're meant to be. Fated mates trump everything."

It takes all I have not to flinch at the mention of other men. I have no right to be upset about it. It's not like I could've expected him to be celibate during the time I was gone. But I'm here now and it's time for us to move forward. Grinning at him, I say, "Indeed we are, *sydämeni,*" and lean in, taking his lips in a kiss that I've only dreamt about for twenty years.

CHAPTER FIVE

If I'm dreaming, please don't let me wake up. Laken is back in my arms, *kissing me.* It's something I've only dreamt about, and I can't believe he's finally here. His black hair is longer, reaching just past his shoulders, and he's a few inches taller but other than that, he hasn't changed a bit. He's still got the muscled build and the adorable spare-tire softness to his middle that's a complete contradiction to the size of his pecs and biceps. The things he's been through...gods I can't even imagine how he felt. Being captured, torn away from the people he loved, and stuck in a tank for years...if it were me, I don't think I could've survived. *He's so strong.* Ending the kiss, I stare into his perfect blue eyes and say, "Come on, let's go up to the house and you can tell me all about this Widow person." *Such an odd name for someone.*

Laken laughs and pats my chest with his hand. "Let me grab my bag and douse the fire in the pit."

Kissing him one more time, I tell him, "There's a lid that'll smother the fire behind my chair." He nods and heads into the cave. When I found that note this morning, I thought Michael and James were playing a cruel joke on me. I know they're not the type but other than Laken, they're the only ones who knew about the notes we left each other. I remember the day I told them about it. It was the anniversary of his disappearance and the day before Michael and James' wedding.

With the festivities for the wedding going on, I'd been missing Laken way more than usual. After a few too many shots of tequila, I told them everything about him and our relationship. Including the notes. Normally, when sober I'd keep those private details to myself, but tequila scrambles my brain and loosens my tongue. Though thankfully, I managed to keep from confessing the location of our spot. That's something that's ours and always will be. Over the years, when I was feeling particularly lonely and wanting to be close to him, I'd go there and sit for a while. Maybe read a book or just close my eyes and listen to the ocean.

Joke or not, I couldn't ignore the note so, I quickly threw some clothes on and raced down here. *I'm glad I did.* If I'd ignored it, I might've missed my chance to reunite with the love of my life. Maybe it's nuts to want to pick up where we left off, but I can't find it in myself to care. Michael and James might have an opinion about this, *and Stanley too* since we literally just ended things yesterday, but I don't care about that either. This is my life, my choice, and I refuse to lose any more time with him because others don't approve of us jumping right back into things.

Laken's hand brushing over my shoulders pulls me from my musings. Grinning at him, I take his hand in mine and lead him up the path to the house. "Have you been to see your family yet?"

Laken shakes his head. "No. As soon as my plane landed, I came here. Maybe it makes me a horrible person but for years, all I thought about was getting back to you. My family hardly ever crossed my mind. Memories of you and dreams of our life if I ever managed to escape were the only things keeping me sane. I'll go see my family in a few days to let them know what happened and that I'm back. Right now, I just want to enjoy some time alone with you before I throw myself to the wolves."

Barking out a laugh, I bump his shoulder with mine and say, "Come on, your family isn't that bad."

"No, they're just overwhelming. Once they find out I'm home, I won't have a minute's peace until they've gotten all the details of what happened and smothered me to within an inch of my life. You know how my mom is. She'll be feeding me at every opportunity, and I'll gain thirty pounds."

"You have a point."

When we get to the house, I lead him into the kitchen so I can start breakfast. When she was still living, my grandma taught me the basics of cooking. My parents employed a personal chef, and I wasn't allowed into the kitchen with the 'help.' I'd be one of those people that survives on microwavable meals and takeout if it weren't for the summers spent here. I've expanded my knowledge over the years thanks to all the cooking shows I've watched.

Something I'm glad for now that I'm the one responsible for most of our meals. With how bad his right hand shakes and being in a wheelchair, grandpa can't easily cook for himself. The kitchen isn't handicap friendly. He still likes to grill, and I watch him like a hawk when he does it, in case he gets tired and needs me to take over. I thought about having the kitchen remodeled so everything is lower and in reach for him but with the paralysis he'd still need help. I did have one of those chair lift things installed on the stairs so he wouldn't have to move downstairs to the study.

As I'm pulling out ingredients for Dutch apple pancakes, Laken says, "This is gorgeous." Looking over my shoulder, I see him holding up the stained-glass vase I made. The flowers in it have wilted and need to be replaced. I'll have to grab some from the local florist the next time I go to the store. "Thanks, I made it."

Laken's eyes widen. "You made this?"

I nod. "I've got a fine arts degree in glass blowing. My workshop is out back. I'll show it to you later."

"That's amazing. You're very talented."

Blushing, I tell him, "Thanks. I tried the corporate thing like my parents wanted but it wasn't me. After you disappeared, I didn't want to be here, so I went to college and got that business degree. I came back five years later when grandpa broke his leg and needed help around here. When he was healed, I stayed so he could retire."

Laken looks around and asks, "Where is your grandpa? I remember him being up and ready to start his day by now."

Sighing, I give him a sad smile and say, "Grandpa had a stroke recently. It left him paralyzed on his left side. Add in the fact that he's eighty-five and he's not as spry as he used to be. I've got at least another hour before he'll be up. I'll help him through his morning routine before bringing him breakfast. His nurse will be here about that time too."

Laken comes around the island and wraps his arms around me. "Jesus, *sydämeni,* I'm sorry to hear that."

Hugging him tight, I breathe in his scent. I don't know if it's his soap or just him, but it reminds me of a mint julep cocktail. "It's okay. We've gotten used to our new normal and I enjoy taking care of him. God knows my parents couldn't be bothered. They wanted to stick him in a home!" The thought is completely abhorrent to me, and it shows in my tone.

Laken growls, "Assholes."

"Yeah, sometimes I wonder how it's possible for my father to have come from my grandpa and grandma. They're nothing alike. My mother's the same. Her parents were the nicest people."

Laken nods. "I remember them from all those family barbeques you brought me to. What happened to them?"

"It was an accident. Happened the year after you disappeared. They were on their way home from seeing a play. It was raining, a drunk driver crossed into their lane, and they drove off a bridge."

"Fuck that's awful. I'm sorry I wasn't here for you."

"Don't be. You would've been here if you could. It wasn't your fault that you weren't. Now, I'm going to start breakfast."

Laken smiles at me. "Need any help?"

Nodding, I hand him a knife and say, "You can peel and slice the apples while I mix up the batter."

Laken kisses my cheek and gets to work. It's such a domestic thing, cooking together. Something I've hoped to experience with my partner, and I can't stop myself from smiling as I start pouring the batter ingredients into a mixing bowl. A knock on the front door followed by it opening, draws my attention. Michael and James' voices travel down the hall, and I resist the urge to groan. Of course, they'd stop by this morning...I'm sure Michael told James exactly what he said to me last night and now they're here to make sure I'm okay. Which is the last thing I need right now.

I'd hoped to enjoy a nice breakfast with Laken, just the two of us, catching up and learning about each other again. I have questions about him being a shifter and our mating. If it's the same as what I've read in books or different. *I still want to know who Widow is and how they helped him so I can send them a gift as a thank you.* With the arrival of my friends, I have a feeling I'll be spending the morning fighting with them instead.

Leaning over, I hurriedly whisper, "My friends are here and once I introduce you, they're probably going to blow up, so brace yourself."

Laken winks at me and says, "If I can handle rowdy bikers fighting over who gets the last piece of chocolate cake, I can handle your friends."

Chuckling, I kiss his cheek and say, "You're telling me that story later."

Laken laughs. "It's not much of a story. A couple of Widow's friends were having a debate about who should get the last piece of chocolate cake when we arrived. It looked like it was about to come to blows so, I got in between them, grabbed a knife and cut the piece of cake in half. They both got a piece and there was nothing left to argue about. I'd planned to just take it and run while they were distracted because I haven't had cake in years but decided it was in my best interest to diffuse the situation, not potentially get my ass kicked by a couple of angry bikers."

Barking out a laugh, I kiss his lips, "I'll make you a cake, *rakkaani*. I'll make you all the cakes." *So, Widow's a biker...that's interesting.*

Michael clears his throat and says from behind me, "Um...Ferris? What's going on here?"

CHAPTER SIX

I hope this doesn't turn into a fight. The last thing I want is to come between Ferris and his friends. Ferris picks up the bowl of ingredients and starts mixing them before turning to face his friends. With a grin, Ferris says, "Morning guys. What's going on is, I'm making Dutch apple pancakes for breakfast. Are you joining?"

The beefcake's eyes narrow. "You know that's not what I meant." He gestures between Ferris and me and says, "Who is this guy? You seem pretty cozy. Especially since you only ended things with Stanley yesterday."

The twink-like guy looking a little worse for wear, moves around the beefcake to sit at the bar. His scent reaches my nose and I wonder if Ferris knows his friend is a vampire. *Likely not.* While the beefcake and Ferris are in a stare down, I ask the twink, "Would you like anything to drink?"

"Coffee. No sugar, no milk. I need it to wake me up and flush the alcohol from my system." With a groan, he rubs his head and mutters, "I shouldn't have had that twelfth pink poodle."

Okay...I have no idea what a pink poodle is but I'm going to assume it's a cocktail because I don't even want to think of the other implications behind that name. Turning to the coffee pot, I pick up the full pitcher and pour it into one of the mugs from the hanger above it. The coffee pot must be on a timer because it was already done when we walked in. Sliding the cup to the twink, I say, "Here you go."

The twink pulls the mug to him, takes a sip and sighs. "Thanks. I'm James by the way. The stud-muffin I arrived with is my husband, Michael. And you are?"

"Laken. Nice to meet you."

At the mention of my name Michael shouts, "What? Laken? As in the same Laken who disappeared twenty years ago?"

I nod and Michael turns to Ferris. "Are you fucking nuts? He disappears, breaks your heart, and now that he's shown up you act like none of that even happened? What is wrong with you?"

Ferris growls, "Keep your voice down! My grandpa doesn't need to be woken by your screeching this early. There's nothing wrong with me. Laken explained why he disappeared, and I've accepted it. I never stopped loving him. As far as I'm concerned, the twenty years we spent apart are part of the past. We're moving forward together. If you can't accept that, you can leave."

Michael's shoulders sag and he rubs his face with his hands. "I don't understand."

James pipes in with, "You're mates, aren't you?"

Michael hisses at James, "What are you doing, J?"

James waves him off and points to me. "Laken's a shifter. If I were him and spent twenty years away from my mate, I'd waste no time in telling him all about what I am and what we mean to each other when I saw him again. We can let the cat out of the bag."

Ferris nods. "He's right, Michael. The big reveal of his animal half was part of Laken's explanation. If I didn't understand the need for secrecy, I'd be upset with the two of you for keeping the fact one or both of you are paranormals to yourselves. You know how much I love paranormal romances."

James laughs. "We know and honestly, we probably would've told you in a few more years because you'd notice we aren't aging, and we have no plans to move on from this place. I'm honestly surprised you hadn't figured it out already. This entire peninsula is ninety percent paranormal. The other ten percent are humans in the know about us."

Ferris shrugs and chuckles self-deprecatingly. "Apparently, I'm slow on the uptake."

Michael glares at me and asks, "If you're Ferris' mate, why did you leave him? I thought all paranormals are wired to cherish their mates. Yet you rejected yours."

Growling at him, I grip the counters to keep myself from flying across the counter at him like I desperately want to. "Fuck you, and the high horse you rode in on, asshole. I did not reject him. I didn't even know Ferris and I were mates back then. I suspected it, but I wasn't sure. It's not my fault I was kidnapped while swimming, trapped in my animal form, stuck in a tank and then sold to a curiosity show where I've been the source of human entertainment for the past twenty years. I never would've abandoned him like that."

Turning my back, I refocus on cutting up the apples for the pancakes before I give into the urge I have to strangle Ferris' friend. A hand on my shoulder has me tensing, since it isn't Ferris doing the touching. Michael says, "I'm sorry, Laken. I shouldn't have jumped to conclusions about you. I don't want to see Ferris get hurt again. He's my best friend and he's been nursing his broken heart for years. I've never seen him truly happy. I thought that might change when Stanley lasted longer than anyone else did, but I was wrong. I didn't know the full story and I should've gotten it from you first instead of acting like an asshole and assuming you'd come back into his life only to leave again and we'd have to pick up the pieces."

Nodding in understanding I tell him, "I swear, you don't have to worry about me hurting him. I'm not going anywhere ever again. Not without him at my side."

"That's all I needed to know. I hope in the future, we can be friends."

Pointing to the bar with the knife, I tell him, "I'd like that. Now, have a seat. You and James are staying for breakfast." Then addressing Ferris, I say, "Bring your grandpa down to join us when the food is ready. He shouldn't have to eat alone."

Ferris winks at me and says, "You got it, *rakkaani.*"

Ferris and I work together to finish preparing breakfast. Ten minutes before it's ready almost an hour after starting, Ferris heads upstairs to change clothes and help his grandpa get ready to come down to eat. The time between the moment Ferris told me about his grandpa's stroke to now is nowhere near enough to have prepared myself for the sight of him when Ferris returns. Gone is the larger-than-life man who always had a pep in his step and a candy in his pocket for us kids. He's been replaced by a much frailer counterpart. His once salt and pepper hair is now snow white and he's lost most of the muscles built by years of hard work. There's a canula in his nose supplying oxygen and the left side of his face is sagging a bit, likely an after-effect of the stroke.

It hurts my heart to see the spry sixty-five-year-old man I remember reduced to this. Logically, I know this is what happens as humans get older, but it doesn't make it hurt less. I've always thought of him like he was my own grandpa and I hate that I was robbed of so much time. Time I could've spent with him and Ferris. *If I ever get my hands on the people responsible for my captivity, I'll make them wish they'd never been born.* When grandpa sees me, his eyes light up and the right side of his mouth tilts up in a smile.

"Laken, you're back," is how he greets me, but it comes out sounding more like, "Lay you back."

Grinning at him, I lean down and hug him. "Hi pops. I missed you."

He hugs me back as hard as he can, which isn't very. "Missed you too."

Finally releasing him, I say, "Come on, pops, let's get you seated at the table. I helped make Dutch apple pancakes for breakfast so you're in for a treat."

Ferris snorts out a laugh. "Every day is a treat for him." Then he leans in and whispers conspiratorially, "I spoil him with semi-healthy comfort foods for breakfast, so it softens the blow of the completely healthy lunch and dinners he has to eat."

Pinching his cheek, I coo, "You're such a good grandson."

Ferris sticks his tongue out at me and pushes grandpa's wheelchair over to the dining table. Michael moves some chairs over to make room for grandpa's chair to go under the table. While they're getting grandpa settled, I start carrying the food to the table. James has already laid out plates, napkins, and silverware for us. As soon as I have all the food on the table, I go back for the coffee carafe, juice pitcher and all the condiments, placing them on the table with the food.

With everything on the table, I take the seat next to Ferris, who is sitting by grandpa. We serve ourselves and dig in. As we eat, Michael and James tell me stories about Ferris. Things I've missed over the years. I almost choke on my food from laughing when they tell me about the Halloween incident. By the time all the food is gone, my sides are hurting because I laughed so much. Grandpa seemed to enjoy himself even though he didn't speak much. You could tell by the light in his eyes. Now that I'm back, I'll make sure to spend as much time with him as I can.

As I'm helping Ferris clear the table, Michael asks, "So, Laken, what are your plans, now that you're back?"

Shrugging, I tell him, "I haven't really thought about it. My only plans when I got on the plane were to come here, work things out with Ferris and see my family to let them know I'm okay. Beyond that? I have no idea. I don't know if I want to go back to working on my family's boat as a fisherman or if I want to take the time to learn to do something else. I've got time to figure it out though, so it's not a priority."

Ferris chimes in with, "And I have enough money to support us both if Laken decides he'd rather not do anything."

Shaking my head, I smile at Ferris. "I appreciate the gesture, *sydämeni,* but I'm not the type to freeload."

Ferris raises an eyebrow at me and asks, "Do you think stay at home dads or moms are freeloaders?"

"No, but that's different. We don't have kids. There's no reason for me to stay at home and not work."

Ferris says, "We have grandpa. Yes, he has a nurse but I'm sure he'd love more company. He's a good reason to stay at home and not work."

Grumbling, I bump his shoulder with mine and say, "You have a point. I've already missed so much time with him. I don't want a job to get in the way and cause me to miss more."

Ferris grins smugly. "Then it's settled. You can spend all the time you want with grandpa and can worry about getting a job later." *After he's gone* goes unsaid but I know it's what he's thinking, and it makes my heart ache. If there was a way to keep the old man around for a long time, I'd do anything to make it happen, but I know there's nothing. As much as I hate it, it's the circle of life and there's nothing I can do to change it. Unless by some miracle, grandpa ends up being the mate to a paranormal and gets claimed. I've heard stories of elderly human mates having the signs of their age reversed after being claimed by a paranormal. It's a nice thought but there's a slim chance of it ever happening. A guy can wish though.

After we've finished the dishes and seen Michael and James off, I turn to Ferris and ask, "So, what's the plan for today?"

Ferris grins at me with a feral gleam in his eyes and says, "I can think of a few things, but that'll be for later. Grandpa is in such good spirits, I'd like to take him out for a walk, maybe head into town for lunch. Get him out of the house for a while since he spends almost all of his time here these days."

Kissing him softly, I say, "Let's do it. But if we see my family, we're going in the opposite direction. I don't want to spend the day explaining myself to them."

Ferris winks. "You got it, *rakkaani*."

"Then let's get out of here."

After sending a text to grandpa's nurse about where we'll be going, Ferris gets grandpa, and we head out. There's a ramp on the front porch that leads to a wood plank path that splits in three directions. Toward the lighthouse, the beach, and our spot. Ferris pushes grandpa's chair, and we walk the path to the beach that's in the opposite direction of our spot. Going this way, we can pick up the boardwalk and make our way to town. At least, that's how it used to be. *I hope it hasn't changed.* Seeing the town for the first time in so long is bound to be a shock as I'm sure things have changed. However, it

would be nice if some things are still the same.
Maybe then I won't feel so out of sorts. Like I don't
know anything about the place I call home anymore.
Guess we'll see, won't we?

CHAPTER SEVEN

In twenty years, the town hasn't changed much. Sure, some shops have closed when the owners packed up and moved on, and some new buildings have been added but other than that, almost everything is exactly as it was. Most of Valtameri's population being paranormals certainly explains a lot. Like how there are so few elderly folks and how shops that have been open since before my parents were born are still owned and operated by the same people. Now that I know the truth, I can't believe I didn't put two and two together before. Its glaringly obvious now, that something isn't quite what it seems with this town. Kind of makes me feel like a dumbass for not noticing sooner. Then again, I haven't exactly been paying attention since Laken disappeared. It's like I've lived in a fog, going through the motions of existing but not actually living.

When we get into town, Laken visibly relaxes, and a smile crosses his face. I didn't realize how tense he was until now. Raising an eyebrow at him, I ask, "You okay, *rakkaani*?"

He nods as his grin widens. "I am now. I thought I wouldn't recognize anything after being away so long. I'm glad that isn't the case."

"Some things are different but it's not the drastic change I can imagine you were picturing."

"I'm not saying it's rational, but I was a little afraid that if I didn't recognize this place then maybe I didn't belong here anymore. That I had no right to call it home."

"That's nonsense," I reassure him vehemently. "You were born here. It doesn't matter where you go, for how long, or if you don't recognize a damn thing when you come back, this will always be your home. Home is where the heart is, *rakkaani*, and yours is here."

Laken's eyes dance with mirth and his lips twitch. "You always did have a way with words, *sydämeni*." His tone is teasing, and I wink at him in return. The sidewalks lining main street are busier than usual so visiting each shop for Laken to reacquaint himself with the town is a slow-going process that takes a few hours. By the time we've visited the last one and have bought a few things, my stomach feels like it's ready to eat itself, so we head to a restaurant for lunch. The excursion has tired grandpa out, so instead of eating in like I'd planned, we get our meal to-go and head home.

When we get back, we eat at the dining table with Michelle. I made sure to grab her something so she wouldn't have to cook for herself and eat alone. Laken tells her some of my more embarrassing moments as a child. Like the time I went swimming in the ocean and came out with a crab dangling from my swimsuit perilously close to the goods and started screaming 'get it off' while hopping around trying to shake it off. Michelle is laughing so hard tears are streaming down her face.

Grandpa is laughing too, and it makes my heart happy. Getting him to laugh or even crack a smile has been a hard-fought war ever since the stroke. Grandpa's depressed and I completely understand why but it's getting harder to pull him out of that darkness. Today has been the happiest I've seen him in a long time, and I know it's because of Laken. With Laken back for good, I have a feeling he'll have an easier time succeeding where I couldn't when it comes to pulling grandpa out of the darkness.

After lunch, Michelle takes grandpa upstairs for his afternoon nap, and I clear our trash from the table. When I'm done, I turn to Laken and ask, "Want to see my workshop?"

He grins at me and nods. Taking his hand, I lead him out the back door and down the path to my workshop. Opening the door, I flip on the light, throw my arms out with a flourish and say, "Voila," making him laugh. The laugh dies when he sees the shelves lining one wall where I keep the finished pieces I haven't sold yet. I have another shelf for pieces I'm preparing to pack and ship, and another shelf for the pieces I haven't received final payment on yet. Lining the other wall are cube storage shelves filled with cylinders of glass that I use in my projects. This area of my workshop is climate controlled to protect the integrity of the pieces. At the back of this room is a set of solid insulated doors that keeps the heat from my furnace from affecting the temperature in this front room.

I'm considering opening up a storefront in town to go with the online store I already have but I'm undecided about it. On one hand, I could see the benefits having a storefront could bring, even though it would also mean I'd need to increase my production in order to have enough inventory to stock the store. On the other hand, I like my online store and doing commissioned works so I can pick and choose how much work I do and don't have to stress about it as much. I could probably do one of those pop-up stores that seem to be so trendy nowadays. Maybe rent a space for a couple days, sell my work and then close up shop when the time is up. It's something to think about. I'm in no hurry to decide so I've got plenty of time to get it all figured out.

Laken's awed whisper of, "These are gorgeous," has me blushing to the tips of my ears. It's not that I'm embarrassed or shy about showing my pieces, there's just something about having Laken in my space, complimenting my work that hits all my hot spots like an intimate touch. *Is it hot in here or is it just me?* Resisting the urge to fan myself, I lean against the counter where I do all my packaging and watch Laken walk around, admiring the pieces I've made. I'd explain the inspiration and stories for them, but Laken is flitting from piece to piece faster than I can speak. If I tried, he'd be on his fifth or sixth piece while I'm still talking about the first.

He stops at one shelf and picks up my favorite piece. It's one of the first and a representation of us. Two different colored waves -one blue, one green- crash together in the shape of a heart and merge together in the color turquoise in the middle of a cave mouth. It's one of the few pieces in this room that aren't for sale and never will be. Crossing the room, I wrap my arms around Laken from behind and kiss his neck. "This was one of the very first ones I made after my workshop was built."

Laken stares at the figurine. "It's us, isn't it?"

Hugging him tighter, I nod. "It is. It took me a few tries to get it right. I ended up accidentally breaking three of them before I got the waves into the shape I wanted. Then forming the cave came with another set of challenges. It took six tries to make the rocky details of the cave a perfect match to our spot."

"It's amazing, *sydämeni*. I love it. Why don't you display it in the house?"

"It was my way of keeping you all to myself when you weren't here. That cave has always been our spot and I don't want to share anything about it with anyone else. Besides, I don't want people seeing it and thinking they can buy it from me or commission an exact replica. This is one of a kind and it'll be the only one I ever make."

Laken returns the piece to the shelf and turns in my arms. "I know exactly how you feel, but maybe we can move it to our bedroom so we're still the only ones who see it. It's too beautiful to leave on a shelf out here."

Grinning, I kiss him softly and say, "Whatever you want, *rakkaani*."

One of his hands travels up my chest to my neck where he runs a finger under the collar of my shirt. The touch sends a shiver of arousal through me, and I can't wait any longer. I've been in a semi-aroused state since the kiss we shared on the beach this morning and now that we're alone, I want him to claim me. To make me his and tie us together permanently. I never want to experience the loss of him again and with the bond, I'll never have to. At least, that's what I'm hoping will happen. I haven't asked him what it means to be the mate of a paranormal. I'm going off what I've read in books, and I could be way off. *I should ask him before we go further.*

Looking into his eyes, I ask, "Can you tell me what's going to happen with us? I know you said paranormals and fated mates were real, like in my books, but is everything exactly the same? How does bonding work?"

Laken nods. "All fiction has some basis on truth, *sydämeni.* Bonding between paranormals and their mates is done with an exchange of blood during sex." He touches the spot between my neck and shoulder and purrs, "I'll bite you here when I come inside you then I'll cut myself so you can drink my blood. I know it sounds gross but it's how we'll seal our bond. Once it's in place, your life will extend to match mine. Your aging will slow, your bones will be harder to break, and you'll never get sick. I won't be able to get it up for anyone else and neither will you. We'll be one hundred percent faithful to each other and have centuries together. If we're blessed with a mind link, we'll always be able to communicate even when we're apart for any reason."

I'm relieved it's the same. In my heart, I know he'd never cheat but it'll be nice having that added protection. Stepping back, I take his hand in mine and say, "Come with me."

With a nod, Laken lets me lead him out of the workshop and back into the house. I take him upstairs to my room, but only long enough to grab a blanket and a bottle of lube before dragging him out of the house again. My hurried pace makes Laken laugh. "I'd ask what the rush is, but I already know. The scent of arousal coming off you is making me crazy."

When we get to our spot, I lay out the blanket in front of my chair and turn to Laken. A laugh bubbles out of me when I see he's already stripping. Not willing to be outdone, I kick off my shoes and whip my shirt over my head. Dropping my shorts, I kick them aside at the same time as Laken. Fully naked, we launch at each other, lips meeting in a fury and tongues tangling. It's glorious. I lower myself onto the blanket, pulling Laken down on top of me. His hard cock pressed against mine has me moaning into his mouth. Sliding my hands down his back, I grip his ass and press him harder against me.

Laken pulls back, his breath coming in pants. His hands feel like they're everywhere at once. My chest, my abs, my arms. The teasing touches only heighten the arousal I'm feeling. My cock is already leaking, and I feel like I could go off like a rocket at any moment. Laken leans in and kisses his way down my neck and chest teasing my nipples with his tongue before nipping each. *Fuck that feels good.* Laken and I fooled around as teens, but we never got the chance to take things all the way. In the years he's been gone, I never had the desire to go there with anyone else. I'm glad I didn't now. Laken gets to be my first, just like he was my first with everything else when we were younger. I've used toys on myself before, so I know what it feels like but that's all.

Laken's lips wrapping around my cock makes me arch off the blanket. "Laken...oh gods."

He holds out his hand and it takes a minute for my brain to catch on to what he's silently asking for. Grabbing the lube from where I dropped it in my haste to get undressed, I hand it to him. The snick of the cap being opened is like music to my ears. *This is finally happening.* When a lubed finger presses inside me, I moan loudly as an orgasm hits me out of nowhere. If Laken wasn't distracting me with his finger in my ass and my cock still in his mouth, I'd be embarrassed about coming so soon.

One finger becomes two and by the time Laken gets to three, I'm a writhing mess begging him to take me. Laken lets my cock slip from his mouth and I'm surprisingly still hard even after one hell of an orgasm. Laken's fingers leave my body and I whimper in protest. "Please...I need you."

Laken smiles softly and says, "I need you too," as he positions himself. I wrap my legs around him and let my hands roam over every inch of his skin I can reach. "Take me, *rakkaani*. I'm yours."

It's all the permission he needs to push inside me. Finally having him after so long is enough to bring tears to my eyes. Crying during sex isn't exactly sexy, but I'm not the only one getting emotional. Laken is too. His eyes are just as misty as mine as he stares down at me and when he speaks, his voice is filled with awe. "Being with you like this is better than I ever imagined, *sydämeni*. I don't think I'll ever get enough of you."

Gasping as his cock brushes that special spot within me, I say, "I feel the same, *rakkaani*." Moving my hands to cup his cheeks, I pull him in for a kiss. Slipping my tongue into his mouth, I loop one arm around his back to hold him to me, enjoying the bunching of the muscles in his back as he moves. Laken groans into my mouth and picks up the pace.

Each thrust of his cock brushes against my prostate and pushes me closer to the edge of another orgasm. As Laken's thrusts become hurried and erratic, I know he's getting close too.

Breaking the kiss, I pant, "Laken…"

Something in his eyes turns feral, the color going from blue to black and it's all the warning I have before he leans forward and sinks his teeth into my neck. The brief flash of pain makes me yelp but it quickly turns into a moan as pleasure takes over, going straight to my cock. Laken sucks on the wound and it's as if he's sucking my cock, sending me right over the edge. "Laken!" After a couple more thrusts, he stills, and warmth floods my insides. Taking a page out of the books I've read I bite his neck hard enough to draw blood and swallow. Laken shivers and moans as another orgasm hits him. I feel it when the bond between us snaps into place, and I can't stop the goofy grin that crosses my face.

Laken seals the wound on my neck and pulls back, his expression is affectionate as he strokes my cheek. Instead of speaking, I hear his voice in my head.

You're mine forever, sydämeni.

I always have been, rakkaani. This just makes it official.

"I love you."

My eyes feel misty again and I grip his wrist, stroking the back of his hand with my thumb as I lean into the touch. "I love you too. I never stopped."

Laken leans down and presses his lips to mine and we lose ourselves in the kiss until we're ready to go again. To my disappointment, Laken pulls out of me but it's short lived because he hands me the lube and says, "Your turn."

Grinning, I roll us until he's underneath me then get to work making him mine in return.

CHAPTER EIGHT

I wake up to the sound of a phone ringing and it only takes a second to realize the sound is coming from my clothes. Ferris and I fell asleep after round two. Standing up, I walk over to our clothes, the slight twinge in my ass brings a smile to my face. Searching the pockets, I pull out my phone and see I have a missed call from Widow and a ton of texts on our group chat.

Opening the text thread, I scroll back to the start of the new texts and read.

Oscar: We have a problem, guys. Armed goons were waiting for me on the tarmac when the plane landed. I was shot with a tranq dart as soon as the door opened to let me out. Thank the fates

I fell backward instead of
down the stairs. The flight
attendant was quick to drag
me back in and shut the door
before the goons could rush
the plan. Maverick took off
and once we were in the air,
he pulled out a little
device and searched me for
trackers. He found one in my
bicep. I don't remember how
it got there but I assume it
was done when I was knocked
out after being captured. If
I have one, then it's likely
you guys do too. Have it
removed asap and crush it.

Horror fills me as I realize I've probably led these assholes right to Ferris and his grandpa. The feeling only grows when I scroll down and see a message from Jaco.

Jaco: They came for us too,
but it was when we were in
the city looking for someone
to give us a boat ride back
to our family. We evaded
them and assumed they were
tracking us somehow. We
found each other's trackers
and used a pocketknife we

bought to cut them out
before crushing them.

Widow: Do you need any help?
I can have a couple guys
headed your way within the
hour.

Oscar: I'm good. Maverick
stopped to refuel and flew
us into Ireland. We're
holing up with the Belfast
charter until this blows
over and I'm able to go home
without worrying about
getting captured again.

Jaco: We're good too. After
we evaded capture again, we
found someone to take us
home. We're back with our
pod so we're protected.

Widow: Has anyone heard from
Laken?

Jaco: Not since he told
Oscar to enjoy his flight.

Oscar: Jaco's right.

Widow: He didn't answer his
phone when I called. I'm
worried.

The phone rings in my hand again, and I answer it. "I'm fine Widow. I was asleep when you called."

Widow exhales a sigh of relief. "Thank the gods. I'm glad you're okay but it's possible you've got guys coming for you too. I'm going to have Oscar and Maverick get the club's president to send a couple of the Belfast guys out your way to protect you."

"It might be too late for that. If they tracked Oscar, Jaco, and Jordao, they'll already have my location. They could be heading here right now. Which means I need to go rally the troops. This town is full of paranormals that'll come to my aid because I grew up here."

Ferris' arms wrap around my waist, and I lean back against him. Widow says, "Alright. If you change your mind, I'm only a call away."

Nodding, I say, "Thanks Widow. You're a good friend. I'll call you later."

"You'd better."

Ending the call, I turn to face Ferris. "Get dressed, *sydämeni,* we've got to get back to the house. I want to make sure the assholes coming after me haven't beaten us there. If they do anything to your grandpa or Michelle, I'd never forgive myself."

Ferris nods and says, "I'll call James and Michael on the way, they'll come help us and bring a few friends."

Kissing his cheek, I say, "We're going to need all the help we can get," and start pulling on my clothes. I'm not much of a fighter, but I'll try. However, if they hit me with a tranq dart, it'll all be over. Though if they threaten Ferris or his grandpa, I'll sacrifice myself to protect them. *Hopefully, it won't come to that.* After Ferris dresses and makes his phone call, we make our way back to the house. The cavalry is on its way, I just hope they won't arrive too late. As we come over the hill, I see two black SUVs in the driveway.

Even though I know the answer, I say, "I'm going to assume your friends didn't get here that quickly."

Ferris nods sagely. "You'd be right. Come on, let's circle to the back of the house. If we can get into my workshop without being seen, we can grab something to use as a weapon." Ferris jerks me down behind a set of rocks as two men appear on the front porch of the house.

"It's a good plan, *sydämeni,* but I don't think it'll work. They'll have guns, and we'd have to get the drop on all of them without giving ourselves away. With the size of those SUVs, we can expect as many as fourteen people, and I just don't see us being able to surprise attack all of them without getting caught."

Ferris sighs and quickly sends a text, then peeks over the top of the rock before ducking down again. "Okay, new plan...we walk in the front door and stall them until Michael and James get here with help. I'm sure we can hold out for ten minutes. I'd suggest hiding but with the tracker, they'd find us. Though I have to wonder how long they've been here because if it had been longer than a few minutes, they'd have come to the cave instead of the house once they realized you weren't there. I also can't leave grandpa and Michelle to fend for themselves against a bunch of goons."

Nodding in understanding, I stand and put on a brave face. "Let's do this then."

Ferris takes my hand and squeezes it. "I'm with you, one hundred percent. We'll get through this, *rakkaani.* They won't take you from me now that we've found our way back each other."

Not without a fight goes unsaid.

Hand in hand, we continue down the path to the house ready to face the enemy. Instead of hitting us with tranq darts, the two men on the porch wait for us to go into the house before flanking us. Michelle and grandpa are both tied up. Grandpa is tied to his wheelchair and Michelle is tied to a dining chair. Both have silver tape over their mouths. Michelle looks pissed but grandpa seems a bit dazed and confused. *I hope this bullshit didn't cause him to have another stroke.* Neither of them show any outward signs of injury and my shoulders sag with relief.

Ten men with guns are gathered around. Two stand behind grandpa and Michelle. There's the two behind Ferris and me. The rest are surrounding the couch where two people in fancy suits are sitting. One woman, one man. Both with cold eyes and disdain written on their expressions. I recognize them as the owners of the curiosity show I was sold to. The man in the suit barks at one of the goons, "Scan them."

The goon steps forward with a little machine. He runs it over Ferris first then moves to me. When the device passes over my bicep it beeps loudly. *Damn tracker.* The goon steps back and the man in the suit steps forward, a hard glare on his face. He grips my chin in a bruising grip and growls, "You and your friends have given us a lot of trouble. Now that we've got you, it'll only be a matter of time before we catch them too. If you want something done right, you've got to do it yourself."

This close, I'm able to scent him. *Jackal shifter...so that's how they knew.* I know all species have their bad seeds, but this is crazy. A shifter capturing other shifters for human entertainment is mind boggling. Call me naïve but growing up in a place like Valtameri, I'd never been exposed to the evil of the world. *Until now*. I'd still like to know where they got the drugs to keep us in our animal forms.

The woman stands and comes to join the man. She rubs her hand up his arm before resting it on his shoulder. "Tranq him and let's go. If we stay much longer someone is bound to realize something isn't right here." Her scent reveals her to be a witch. *She probably used herbs and a bit of magic to make the drugs.* I wouldn't be surprised if she used other shifters as guinea pigs for the drug.

The man shakes his head and says, "Not yet. I want to know where the others are since their trackers have been lost. They were all together before they split up. He has to know where they would've gone after getting rid of the trackers."

Folding my arms, I glare at him. "I'm not telling you shit."

The woman smiles sinisterly and singsongs, "Oh yes you will."

She starts to recite the words to a spell but before she can complete it, a tiny glowing blue portal appears from above and something black falls through it. There's a loud bang before smoke fills the room making my eyes water and my nose itch. Suddenly, multiple portals open up and people swarm into the house from all directions, surrounding and taking out the gunmen one by one. When the smoke clears, the suits are trussed up and wrapped together with rope from their shoulders to their ankles. Like pigs in a blanket. James is standing next to them, one foot holding them down, filing his nails like a twinky Captain Morgan without the pirate getup and barrel of rum.

Grinning, I say, "Well, you sure know how to make an entrance."

James giggles, "I really do. Are you guys okay?"

I nod. "We're good."

James calls out, "Michelle, grandpa? How about you two?"

I turn to look and see Michelle rubbing her wrists. Her fury is evident on her face. "We weren't hurt but I wish I could've helped kick their asses. They got the drop on me and with their numbers, I figured it was best to go along with them than try and fight."

Ferris and I cross over to her, wrapping her in a hug. "You did the right thing. You kept yourself and grandpa safe and we'll never be able to thank you enough."

Michelle grins and teases, "You could buy me a steak dinner."

Barking out a laugh, I pat her back. "Done."

Michael comes up to us and says, "We'll get these yahoos out of here and on their way to the European council's jail."

"Sounds good. Thanks for getting here so quickly."

Michael pats my arm and says, "That's what friends are for. Though now that you've claimed Ferris, you're family."

A familiar deep voice comes from behind me, "Speaking of family," and I wince. *Well fuck.*

Turning around, I plaster a smile on my face and say, "Hi dad."

CHAPTER NINE

Walking over to my grandpa, I crouch down in front of him and ask, "Are you alright?" He gives me a shaky thumbs up and I sigh in relief. *Thank the gods.* Michelle tips her head in my direction and says, "You should probably go rescue him."

Turning around, I see Laken and his dad standing together. Laken looks like a deer caught in headlights and his father looks pissed. The man is built like a tank. His tree-trunk-like arms are testing the integrity of the tee he's wearing. Hurrying over, I arrive just in time to hear Laken's dad ask, "Where the hell have you been and why am I just finding out you're back? You should've come straight home as soon as you got here."

Now it's Laken who looks pissed. He crosses his arms and glares. "I did come home. To Ferris. He's my fated mate and my home is where he is. I wanted us to have time alone together before I let anyone else know I was back. Being trapped in my animal form as a curiosity show attraction for twenty years gave me plenty of time to think about what I'd do if I ever escaped. Top of the list was seeing Ferris again and praying we could pick up where we left off. I'm sorry if that hurts you but I couldn't go on not knowing if I could have Ferris. As my family, I knew I'd always have you."

Putting my arm around him, I tuck him against my side. Laken's dad deflates like a balloon. With a sigh, he says, "I get it. I may not like it but that's a me problem. I do wish you would've called to let us know you were okay. I'd have kept your mom away for as long as I could, so you'd have time with Ferris."

Laken gives him a look that says 'yeah right' making his dad laugh. I know Laken's mom, and there's no keeping her from doing something when she sets her mind to it. With a wink, Laken's dad says, "I wouldn't have told her you were back at first. She'd have been mad, but she would've gotten over it. With what happened here today, the whole town will know you're back in a matter of minutes. I hope you're prepared for the hurricane that is your mother."

Laken smiles and says, "I'll have to be."

Laken's dad nods. "Good, because I'm sure she's on her way here and if she isn't, she will be."

People start clearing out of the house, taking the intruders with them. Some stop to welcome Laken back to town while others just nod and wave before leaving. When everyone is gone, leaving myself, Laken, his dad, Michelle and grandpa, I finally relax. I've been tense this whole time worried about everyone not arriving in time to save Laken from being taken.

The living room is a mess. Furniture is tipped over, some of it broken from where people fell into it while fighting. There're holes in the wall where missed punches landed and crooked picture frames. Some have fallen off the wall and broken. A couple of my glass pieces are broken as well, and it saddens me a little. Sure, I can remake them, but the new ones won't be the same as the originals. Sighing at the mess, I kiss Laken's cheek before walking over to the closet where I keep the cleaning stuff. I know I won't have it all cleaned up before Laken's mom arrives, but I want to at least try to make the place somewhat presentable.

Yes, I already know his family, but meeting them as his mate is completely different. I shouldn't be nervous about it, but I am.

Laken comes up and takes the broom from me. "Let me help, *sydämeni.*"

Kissing him softly, I smile and say, "Thanks, *rakkaani*."

Michelle and Laken's dad say, "We'll help too."

With the four of us working, we get the living room put back to rights fairly quick. Laken gets Michelle to remove the tracker in his arm even though the people responsible for his capture are going to be sitting in jail cells for a very long time. When the tracker is crushed and tossed in the trash, Michelle takes grandpa upstairs to rest before dinner. After all the excitement, I don't think he'll be eating down here with us tonight. I'm tying up the last trash bag when I hear a car door shutting outside. Seconds later the front door slams open so hard it leaves a hole in the wall making me wince. Laken's mother looks at the hole and says, "I'm so sorry. I'll pay to fix that."

Shaking my head, I smile at her. "Don't worry about it, Mrs. Key, I've got other holes to patch anyways."

Mrs. Key might be a short pixie of a woman at five feet tall, but she can be intimidating as hell. It's the 'mom' look. You know the one. The one moms give when you've done something wrong. Not that I've ever gotten that look from mine, but I've seen Mrs. Key give it to her kids more than once, so I know what it is. Right now, she's giving me that look with her arms crossed. "Ferris Michael VanAllen, how many times have I told you to call me mom?" *Oh shit, she full named me.*

Laken snickers beside me and she levels him with a glare. "Don't think I've forgotten about you Laken Alexander Key. You've got some explaining to do, mister." *Damn...she's really mad. Full naming both of us.*

Laken immediately stops laughing, a sheepish expression on his face. With a finger wave, he says, "Hi mom."

She growls. "Don't you 'hi mom' me. Get your butt over here."

Laken walks over to her slowly looking like he's about to face down a firing squad instead of his mother. When he's within reach, she pulls him into a hug so tight, he turns a little purple. "I missed you, my boy and I'm so glad you're okay, but you aren't off the hook for not letting us know you were home."

Laken's dad says, "Mary, let the boy breathe."

She loosens her grip and Laken gasps in a breath. "I know mom. I would've told you eventually, I just wanted some alone time with Ferris before the family descended on us like a pack of wolves on their next kill."

Her eyes narrow and I'm suddenly shaking in my boots. Not that I'm wearing boots, but still.

"Laken Alexander Key, are you calling us overbearing?"

Laken holds up a hand, his thumb and finger about an inch apart. "Maybe a little. I knew if I told you, I was back, you'd do that thing you do where you hover and stuff me full of food to make sure I'm okay. Nothing would've kept you away. Not even me asking to be left alone for a bit."

She opens her mouth to protest, then sighs. "You're right. That's exactly what I would've done. But that's not an excuse for not letting us know you were okay. We never stopped worrying about where you were."

Laken sighs and nods. "I know. I should've called. I could've omitted my location until I was ready for you to come see me. It's a moot point now. Where's everyone else? I would've thought you'd bring the whole family with you."

Mary says, "Your brothers are out on the boat with their kids today while their mates and your sisters are off having a girl's day. I was invited along but decided to spend the day doing my own thing. And by thing, I mean your father."

Laken shouts, "Mom, I didn't need to know that," and his dad doubles over laughing.

I missed this. Laken's mom has always been blunt to the point of oversharing but without Laken around, things haven't been the same. *That'll change now*. When the laughter stops, Laken rolls his eyes and says, "tell me about the kids. I want to know everything I missed."

Mary says, "Of course, but first, you're going to tell me everything that's happened with you."

We move to sit on the couch and Laken tells his story from the time he was captured to meeting Widow and everything that came afterwards. When he's done, his parents hug him for a long time before they start regaling him with stories of his brothers meeting their mates and having kids. His sisters are still single, but their dating mishaps are hilarious. His parents don't leave until after we've all had dinner and even then, it takes some convincing to get them out the door.

When their cars disappear down the driveway, I wrap an arm around Laken's shoulders and say, "Well, today was certainly eventful."

"That it was. Let's hope tomorrow isn't. I've had enough craziness for one day."

Barking out a laugh, I nod. "You and me both, *rakkaani*."

Laken takes my hand and links our fingers together, tugging me toward the stairs. Grinning at him, I ask, "Where are you taking me?" As if I don't already know, but it's fun to tease.

Laken winks, "I thought it was obvious, *sydämeni.*"

The image that comes through our mind link has my grin widening.

I like the way you think, rakkaani.

You're going to love the way I think when you're experiencing the reality.

I can't wait.

Then get your sexy ass upstairs.

Laughing, I let go of his hand and run up the stairs with him hot on my heels. As soon as we're through the door of my bedroom, I kick it closed and attack his mouth with mine. *It's going to be a good night.*

EPILOGUE

Carrying the tray of burger patties outside, I head for the grill where grandpa is standing, flipping burgers, looking like a thirty-two-year-old man instead of the eighty-seven he actually is. I was shocked as hell when I came in from working on the lighthouse for lunch and saw him in the kitchen kissing Michelle. If I hadn't seen pictures of him at a young age, I wouldn't have known who he was. Even more surprising was that Michelle's a selkie/witch hybrid.

All those hours Michelle spent with my grandpa, were used to woo him until he allowed her to cast a spell that would reverse his paralysis so they could be together. I didn't need any more details after hearing that. I know how bonding works and didn't want the image of my grandpa getting it on in my head. I thought it was a longshot that he'd be a paranormal's mate and would meet them, but fate proved me wrong. We had to fake his death and remake his identity as my long-lost uncle so my parents wouldn't be suspicious. Not that they even showed up for the funeral. *Assholes*. They sent flowers though.

I'll have many more years with my grandpa around thanks to my new grandma. When I called Michelle granny for the first time she threatened to cut off my favorite appendage if that word ever left my mouth again. I laughed. With what I plan to do today, I'm glad to have them here especially, since I'd been worried grandpa wouldn't live to see it. The ring has been burning a hole in my pocket for weeks now. I've been waiting for the right moment to propose and decided that today, the second anniversary of his return to me would be perfect.

I've invited everyone we know and love to a cookout that'll double as an engagement party. *If he says yes.* I'm not worried about his answer. Our bond means we're basically married anyways but I still want that piece of paper. I want everything with Laken, including kids. Setting the burgers down next to the grill, I ask grandpa, "Is everyone here?"

He nods. "We're just waiting on the man of the hour to arrive."

Laken decided to go back to working the family business. He's captain of his own boat, just like his brothers are. Laken was out on the water today. His brothers brought their boats in early to get here before Laken did so, he'll be the last one to arrive. I decided to stick with my online store instead of opening a storefront because I wanted to have time to spend with any kids we have. Laken and I have talked about it many times. We're going to get a surrogate, but that'll come after the wedding.

Clapping my grandpa on the shoulder, I say, "I'm going to go greet everyone," and make my way to the group of guys in leather standing with another group of guys in regular clothes. I've thanked Widow and his friends over the phone many times. Even sent them a gift basket and some glass pieces I'd made to represent them. However, I still feel like it's not enough. There's no way to express how grateful I am for them helping Laken. I wouldn't have him if it weren't for them.

Smiling, I say, "Hey guys, thanks for coming," when I reach the group.

Widow turns to me and says, "We wouldn't have missed this. Thanks for having us."

"No problem. You guys mean a lot to Laken. Of course, I'd want you here." I invited the entire San Antonio charter and Belfast charter of the Grim Knights as well as Laken's friends, Oscar, Jaco,

Jordao, and their mates. Add in our other friends and family, including Stanley, his vampire mate Ephraim, Michael, and James, and there's at least seventy-five people in the backyard. Grandpa and Michelle have been cooking up a storm all day, preparing side dishes and finger foods for everyone.

Laken's voice comes through our mind link, making me smile.

Umm...sydämeni, why are there like a hundred vehicles in the driveway?

Come to the backyard and find out, rakkaani.

Cupping my hands around my mouth, I shout to everyone, "He's here!"

Everyone immediately goes quiet, and we wait patiently for Laken to appear around the corner of the house. I move so I'm standing alone in the center of the yard. We don't have to wait long. Laken comes around the corner wearing a black t-shirt, under a red flannel long sleeve, blue jeans and black boots. A black beanie covers his long black hair. *Damn he looks delicious.* It's colder on the ocean than it is here. When he reaches me, Laken's got a big grin on his face. "*Sydämeni,* what is all this?"

"It's a celebration."

Laken raises an eyebrow. "Of what?"

Taking his hand in mine, I say, "Of us," and lower to one knee, pulling the box from my pocket and flipping it open to reveal the platinum bands inside. Laken's eyes widen comically, and I start my speech, "Laken Key, I've loved you since we were ten and I didn't understand that's what I was feeling. Even when you were gone, I never stopped loving you. You're my moon and stars. My sun, my sky, and my sea. You're the air that I breathe. You're everything. Please say you'll make me the happiest man alive and be my husband too, *rakkaani*."

Tears stream down Laken's face but he's smiling. With a laugh, he nods furiously, "Yes. Of course, I'll marry you."

Letting out a loud whoop, I jump up and wrap my arms around him, spinning him in a circle. Taking the ring from the box, I slip it on his finger, and take his mouth in a kiss. When we pull apart, I turn so we're facing our guests who are clapping, cheering, and letting out wolf whistles. Throwing our joined hands in the air, I shout, "Let's celebrate!"

The End

I hope you enjoyed Laken and Ferris' story as much as I did writing it. Laken and Ferris have become one of my favorite couples. They were so sweet. If you haven't guessed, there'll be a brand-new series featuring the Grim Knights coming soon. I'd planned to introduce the MC in another book, but Widow and his friends foiled those plans. Thank you so much for reading and keep an eye out for my next book.

Continue reading for the blurb of one of my upcoming books titled

The Vampire's Special Grizzly.

Book ten in the Asphalt Bay Pack series.

The Vampire's Special Grizzly

blurb subject to change

(This story is part of an interconnecting series that was written with the intention of being read in a certain order.)

Alaric Glazkov is the vampire drummer for the band The Dead Tuesdays by night and a video game programmer by day. After aiding in the battle against the dark coven, life is getting back to normal for him and the rest of his friends. The only problem? He's the last single guy in their group. Feeling like the tenth wheel whenever they go out, Alaric longs for someone to call his own now that meaningless sex is no longer doing it for him.

Teagan Spade is a grizzly bear shifter and former special forces operative turned council guardsman. Tasked with protecting two councilmen, Teagan accompanied Krealik and Valik into battle. Now that the fight is over and the councilmen are settled with their mates and staying close to Asphalt Bay, a place full of mated couples, Teagan is faced with his own loneliness.

When an overzealous fan from the past resurfaces Alaric decides to hire a bodyguard and Teagan comes highly recommended by Councilman Krealik. When the two men learn they're mates, the realize there's more at stake than they thought.

*(**Warning:** Contains graphic sexual content and explicit language. Not recommended for those under the age of 18.)*

PLAYLIST

Breathe Underwater—Bullet For My Valentine

The Best—Tina Turner

Good As You—Kane Brown

PLAYLIST

It Only Hurts—Default

Here Without You—3 Doors Down

Love Walked In—Thunder

ACKNOWLEDGEMENTS

I want to thank my parents for supporting me no matter what I do and tolerating me when I get in the zone of writing and ignore them completely. By tolerating, I'm really saying thanks for putting up with my shit. You have no idea how much that means to me. I love you guys. I want to thank Lisa Oliver, one of my favorite authors for encouraging me to write the story speaking in my head instead of forcing myself to stick to a different stereotype and for being an amazing friend I can bounce crazy ideas off of.

I want to thank Jemma Brown for designing such amazing covers for me. I thank the readers for taking the time to read a story from an unknown author like me when I was first starting out. I want to thank my characters for coming to me when I was at a loss as to what to write/do next. Last, of all I want to thank all the musicians out there for playing their music and inspiring me.

ABOUT THE 

Well, Ezra isn't my real name obviously, but I liked the name, so I decided to use it. I live at home with my four dogs and one cat. I started out writing hetero romance novels, but it wasn't where my heart lied. I adore all things paranormal and M/M is by far my favorite genre, so I decided to start writing Paranormal Romances. There's a guaranteed happy ending with each of my books even if it may take some time for my guys to get there. I love each and every character on the page as if they were my own children.

It sounds weird but that's how I feel about them. I've been writing for as long as I can remember but only started actively pursuing it as a career in 2014. Since I published my first book in 2014, I have written and released multiple books with many more to come. My current list of projects is longer than my arm, so I look forward to writing and creating new stories for my readers to enjoy.

OTHER BOOKS BY

Ezra Dawn

Standalones (M/F) *No longer available*

Playboy

The Crimson Deceit

Don't Fear the Reaper

The Boy Next Door

Standalones (M/M)

Paying for Love

Law of the Irish

Practical Ghosters

Abominable What-A?

The Cursed Prince

A Raven Walks Into A Bar *Spin-Off*

The Surgeon's Instant Family *Spin-Off*

Not A Snowball's Chance in Hell

Accidental Valentine

Poke His Bear

A Silver Reckoning

Admirer's Halloween *Spin-Off*

The Warden's Easter Trap

The Keeper's Lost Love — *(You just finished it!!!)*

Asphalt Bay Pack Series (M/M)

An Alpha for the Demigod

The Enforcer's Secret Vampire

The Beta's Poison Bite

Taming the Feral Tiger

The Doctor's Demon Prince

The Leopard's Twin Troubles

The Warlock's Beautiful Bird

The Demon's Gruff Councilman

The Councilman's Miniature Companion

The Four Horsemen Collection (M/M)

The Four Horsemen

Azazel

Sen

Taz

The Graveyard Shift (M/M)

The Mortician

The Caretaker

The Director

The Florist

The Mistake *Spin-Off*

The Driver

The Ghost

Venetian Hills (M/M)

The Alpha's Master

The Second's Cursed Mate

The Beta's Second Chance

The Panther's Favorite Bully

The Demon's Mythical Birds

Risqué Business (M/M)

Be My Prince

Seeking Rayne

The Lion's Crown

Ashes of Phoenix

Paranormals of Rockydale (M/M)

Misunderstanding His Mate

The Friendly Ghost's New Beginning

Forbidden Loves (M/M)

All is Fair in Love and War

The Submission Trilogy (M/M)

The Hybrid's Submission

The Wolf's Hybrid Dom

The Hybrid's Dominant Mate

Furry Tails (M/M)

Sugar and Spice

Crimson and Clover

Watson and Sherlock

Snow and Hail

Diary of a Hitman (M/M)

Blood and Bullets

Past and Poison

Love and Lethal

Planet Xenos (M/M)

The Heir's Vampire Guardian

Boxsets (M/M)

Asphalt Bay Pack Vol. 1

Asphalt Bay Pack Vol. 2

The Graveyard Shift Vol. 1

Upcoming Releases:

Titles Subject to change

Death and His Necromancer—TBA

The Artist's Prickled Fancy -TBA

CONTACT THE 

You can find me on Facebook, MeWe, Twitter, and on my website.

Facebook: Ezra Dawn Author or Ezra's Book Groupies

MeWe: Amanda Ezra Ezra Dawn or Ezra's Asphalt Baywatchers

Twitter: @graveshadowcrow

Website: www.ezradawnauthor.com

I look forward to hearing from you!

Want updates on my new releases, WIP's, and exclusive giveaway opportunities? Sign-up for my newsletter by following this link and filling out the form.

Newsletter: www.ezradawnauthor.com/contact